Kids

Choose You

"I like how your adventures branch off like a tree, which sometimes ends in death—oh well, better start again!"
Winton Parker, age 10

"I like looking down at the bottom of the page and see what's coming up next."
Ahn Jacobson, age 11

"I like how they make you feel like you are the Chief of Operations."
Shannon McDonnell, age 10

"I liked how some choices were short and funny and some were long and had consequences. All the adventures are interesting."
Elizabeth Clark, age 12

Watch for these titles coming up in the *Choose Your Own Adventure*® series.

Ask your bookseller for books you have missed or visit us at cyoa.com to learn more.

1 THE ABOMINABLE SNOWMAN by R. A. Montgomery
2 JOURNEY UNDER THE SEA by R. A. Montgomery
3 SPACE AND BEYOND by R. A. Montgomery
4 THE LOST JEWELS OF NABOOTI by R. A. Montgomery
5 MYSTERY OF THE MAYA by R. A. Montgomery
6 HOUSE OF DANGER by R. A. Montgomery
7 RACE FOREVER by R. A. Montgomery
8 ESCAPE by R. A. Montgomery
9 LOST ON THE AMAZON by R. A. Montgomery
10 PRISONER OF THE ANT PEOPLE by R. A. Montgomery
11 TROUBLE ON PLANET EARTH by R. A. Montgomery
12 WAR WITH THE EVIL POWER MASTER by R. A. Montgomery
13 CUP OF DEATH by Shannon Gilligan
14 THE CASE OF THE SILK KING by Shannon Gilligan
15 BEYOND ESCAPE! by R. A. Montgomery
16 SECRET OF THE NINJA by Jay Leibold
17 THE BRILLIANT DR. WOGAN by R. A. Montgomery
18 RETURN TO ATLANTIS by R. A. Montgomery
19 FORECAST FROM STONEHENGE by R. A. Montgomery
20 INCA GOLD by Jim Becket
21 STRUGGLE DOWN UNDER by Shannon Gilligan
22 TATTOO OF DEATH by R. A. Montgomery
23 SILVER WINGS by R. A. Montgomery
24 TERROR ON THE TITANIC by Jim Wallace

"Yeah. I'm worried about them. It's a risky hike to the sea over these hills, and they can't even see it from where they've landed. They'll need food."

"I hear you, Isabel. We'll hang for a while. Hey, get our club on the radio. If we can contact them we might get a rescue operation going from here," you suggest.

"Righto, commander, good plan."

"This is Delta Tango 23114 calling base. Can you read me?" Isabel's voice says over the intercom.

Silence.

"Repeat, This is Delta Tango 23114 calling base operations at Arbor Field. Please respond," she goes on.

Silence.

"Hey, this is not good," she says. You can hear frustration in her voice.

"Maybe nobody's there yet," you say. The club is just that, a club. The people who man the operations shack are volunteers.

"Try and call that commercial landing field in Red River," you suggest. "There's sure to be someone there." You've raised the Arcus to about three thousand feet while keeping an eye on your friends on the ground below.

Turn to page 25.

For Anson, Ramsey,
Beca, Avery, and Lila.
And Shannon

BEWARE and WARNING!

This book is different from other books.

You and YOU ALONE are in charge of what happens in this story.

There are dangers, choices, adventures, and consequences. YOU must use all of your numerous talents and much of your enormous intelligence. The wrong decision could end in disaster—even death. But, don't despair. At anytime, YOU can go back and make another choice, alter the path of your story, and change its result.

Your love of flying has taken you up in a motor glider more than once, but you're by no means a pro. In your first trans-country flight, you and your copilot Isabel are horrified to see your friends' plane crash over the Baja peninsula! You've had experience flying, but nothing can prepare you for the struggles in the air, on the land, and even in the sea. You're going to meet some strange characters out here in the desert, so you and Isabel had better stick together—it's going to take a lot of strength and good decisions from you both!

"Watch out!" you yell, throwing yourself to the ground just as a glider swoops down on the landing field, dangerously close to you. "Is that guy crazy or something?" you say, picking yourself up from the dry, sandy soil. At the far end of the field, the glider finally jounces to a rough landing. It rumbles awkwardly off the strip and onto the shrubbed terrain along the side of the runway.

"Lucky, I'd say," Isabel Mossberg comments from the operations shack, where your group, the Arbor Field Soaring Club, keeps its office. "Probably a crosswind problem. Look at the wind sock—it's blowing across the runway."

Your eyes follow her pointing hand, where the wind is coming at an obvious forty-five degree angle to the field.

Turn to page 2.

"Still, that pilot should have been prepared," you say. But you quickly realize that it could have been you in that tough situation up there. A chill runs down your spine. You shrug it off, now feeling a little more compassion for the pilot. Landing into the wind is a piece of cake, you think. Crosswind landings are the tough ones.

Isabel is one of your three closest friends at the Arbor Field Soaring Club, along with Josh Buckram and Peter Mosler. The four of you have been friends for a few years.

"Hey, you guys, let's get with it! Time for our preflight planning session. We're leaving soon!" Josh has just come out of the operations shack, a sheaf of papers in his hand.

"Where's Peter?" Isabel asks.

"Right here," says Peter, stepping out into the bright California sunshine after Josh. He is your history teacher at Marlowe High, and he is also your flight instructor. The three of you learned to fly with him last summer. Your shared love of flying created a strong bond between the four of you.

"We can preflight later," Peter says. "Let's look at these maps first."

The four of you move to a picnic table out of the wind. It's still strong enough that you have to use small rocks as weights to hold down the maps and other papers.

"Here's our route to the Baja peninsula. It's over some pretty tough terrain," Josh says, spreading out a map of the region.

Go on to the next page.

"This is serious flying. The Baja peninsula is very remote, and it's bone dry. You make a forced landing there without water on board and you won't last a day," Peter warns.

"You're making me thirsty already," Isabel replies.

"If I ever have to crash-land it's going to be on a beach," Josh offers.

Peter laughs good-naturedly. "Well no one's going to have make a forced landing. Let's get back to the maps. We'll take off at 0900 hours and head due south, a compass heading of 180 degrees. Once we reach an altitude of forty-five hundred feet, we'll cut the power and let the winds take us. Okay?"

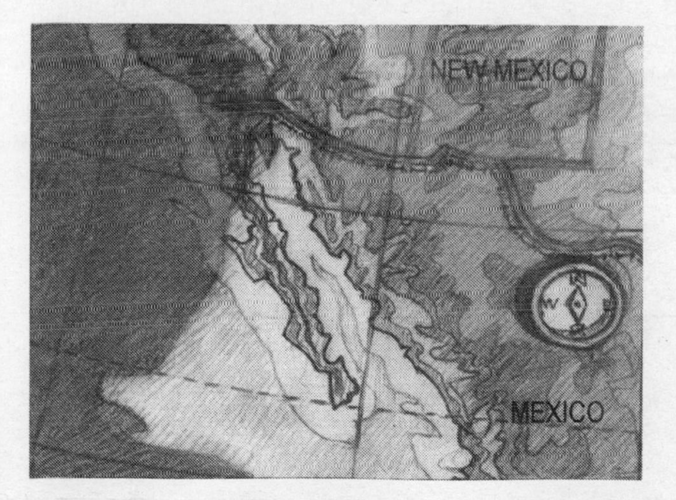

Turn to page 4.

"Sounds good to me," you reply, looking at the maps. "What if we actually do have to go down?" Isabel asks with real concern.

"You always look at the dark side," Josh says softly, busying himself with the weather maps.

"Hey, it's great to be prepared—that's what I taught you," Peter adds.

Today the four of you are taking a long-distance flight in your soaring club's two new motor gliders. These are special gliders equipped with very light engines mounted in the front of the fuselage, and two seats—one behind the other. This is the longest flight you, Isabel, and Josh have ever taken. You know even though Peter is advertising it as fun, it is a test to see if you really have the "right stuff" to be a top qualified pilot. The pressure is on. You'll be piloting one of the silver birds.

It's spring vacation in southern California. The day is clear, hot, and dry. The wind is fresh and out of the northwest. But there is a hint of coming storms—you can feel it in your bones.

Go on to the next page.

"Aren't we leaving kinda late, Pete?" you ask. Usually you leave much earlier in the morning.

"We've got plenty of time. I got permission to land at an old emergency strip just the other side of the Mexico-California border. We're going to set up camp there. It'll be a three-day trip, my friends. I checked it out with your parents. I thought I'd surprise you."

Turn to page 6.

"You mean it? Man, we can spend the night? Cool!" Josh exclaims.

"What are we going to do about food?" you ask. You have a few provisions packed, but not enough for three days.

Peter smiles. You know that smile; it's his teacher's smile, a sneaky smile that says he has all the answers. And he usually does. "We catch our own," he tells you.

"Catch our own what?" Isabel asks suspiciously. "It's one thing to order a hamburger, it's another to kill it."

"Yeah," Josh adds. "Some fun trip you planned for us, Peter."

"Hold on, guys. You aren't giving me a chance. I arranged for a friend to drop off some fishing gear at the airstrip. And just in case we don't catch any fish, I asked him to leave a cache of food for us. The caretaker there is a Señor Gonzales. He'll take care of everything for us. This is going to be lots of fun. You'll like it, trust me."

Turn to page 8.

7

A day later you're reunited with Josh and Peter. The US Border Patrol and the Mexican Federales had been planning a raid on a gang of drug smugglers in the area where you reported the downed Arcus. Josh and Peter were rescued from an encounter with the powerful group just in time, thanks to your radio call reporting their crash.

It feels great to be a hero, and it feels even better to be alive. But what really thrills you is knowing that you've earned your silver wings.

The End

Forty-five minutes later, after giving the aircraft a good preflight check, storing the emergency water rations, and checking the weather and the flight control center in Los Angeles, you and Isabel climb into your silver-winged, red-bodied Arcus 12 motor glider. You taxi out onto the strip. You feel a thrill—the Arcus 12 is your favorite make of motor glider. The sun glints on the black ID code on your silver wing: DT 23114. The Limbach engine is ticking over nicely. The oil and manifold pressure, temperature, and fuel tanks all read A-OK. You waggle the stick to check the ailerons and the elevator and kick the rudder pedals to be sure that control surfaces are functioning.

You are the pilot in command. Isabel sits behind you—she is the navigator. The two of you are connected by radio.

"Let's go down the checklist one more time," you say over the intercom.

"Right," Isabel answers, and the two of you carefully note everything on the list, knowing that there is no room for error in flying.

Right next to you is the other Arcus with Peter and Josh aboard. Josh is the pilot in command.

"Let's go," Peter says over the radio.

"Roger," you reply.

Turn to page 10.

DT 23114
DT 23114

The sleek aircraft hesitates for a minute as the RPMs build. You release the brakes. The plane shudders momentarily, rolls down the dirt strip, and lifts off into the slight morning haze with ease.

Gaining altitude in large circles, you sweep through the sky. There is nothing around you except for the other Arcus with Josh and Peter. The altimeter on the instrument panel climbs slowly but steadily until you reach forty-five hundred feet. Glancing at the instrument panel, you notice the presence of thermals, masses of upward-moving warm air.

These thermals are what your motor glider will ride once the engine is cut. With them you can stay airborne. Without them, your aircraft will slowly lose altitude and have to land.

"Delta Tango 23114 switching engine off," you announce over the radio.

"Read you loud and clear. We're switching off as well," Peter replies.

There is a rush of wind, and then a sense of freedom as the engine dies and the propeller spins in freewheel mode and then stops. The silence is calming.

Two hours later you cross into Mexican airspace, careful to radio your entry to Mexican authorities. They acknowledge and give permission.

Turn to page 14.

It's going to be a long wait. The sun doesn't go down until seven-thirty, and your watch reads 4:31. Looking up at the sky, you notice that the storm has moved quickly down the peninsula and out to sea. It's clear, and the afternoon sun is intense. The rocks give some shade, and you stretch out, ready for the long wait. One thing that keeps you going is the thought that Peter and Josh might arrive back at any time.

You soon begin to regret your decision to wait. You think you should give up and go back to Isabel. The thought of her alone and sick in the Arcus makes you uneasy.

Your thoughts are interrupted by some movement down by the plane. You watch carefully. It isn't Peter or Josh, you find, as a man steps warily into the open. He is armed, and he surveys the area with a careful gaze. Moments later he is joined by a second man who also carries a weapon. One of the men is dark haired, the other is blond. They are both dressed in jeans and khaki shirts.

Instinct tells you that these men are not friendly, so you try to blend in with the rocks. They don't give much protection, but they are comforting in their solidity.

Turn to page 12.

The blond man settles down under the wing of the Arcus, and makes a call on a cell phone, speaking in a low voice. The other man slips around to the rear of the Arcus and disappears into the maze of shrub trees.

You consider several plans. You could circle around behind the plane and follow the man to see if he leads you to Peter and Josh. If so, you had better move quickly. Or you could stay put, wait and watch, and hope that Josh or Peter will turn up.

If you decide to follow the man who just left, turn to page 59.

If you decide to stay put, turn to page 79.

OK85117

"Great, huh?" you say to Isabel, looking at the spiny hills running down the Baja peninsula. The Pacific Ocean glimmers to starboard, the Gulf of California to port.

"I love it," she replies.

Suddenly you hear a crackle of noise on the radio.

"Little problem here. We've got an electrical failure."

It's Josh's voice, and although it sounds calm, you can hear the anxiety in it.

"I read you, Josh. Tell me more," you reply. Both you and Isabel crane your necks to catch a glimpse of their plane, which has dropped several miles astern of yours. You finally spot it as you make a slow banking turn to the left

"I smell burning wiring, but there's no smoke yet. Some of the instruments are already out," he replies.

"Throw the breakers," you suggest.

"We have. No good. We're landing. Better safe than sorry."

"We'll join you," you offer. Isabel signals her assent.

"Okay, but you don't have—" Their radio transmission cuts out.

Anxiously you watch as they spiral down in large circles. The sandy land beneath is rugged.

"We could return to our base after they land and get help, Isabel. Or we could land with them."

"It's a tossup. You're the pilot in command. What do you think?" she replies.

Turn to page 16.

You watch their aircraft descend gracefully, finally meeting the sandy yellow terrain below. You see it skid and then come to an abrupt halt, tipping over on its port wing. You're tempted to land and pick Josh and Peter up, but landing where they are would be a difficult maneuver. The landing area is narrow, and on either side the ground is rough and rocky. Worse, there's a strong crosswind blowing.

Even if you landed successfully, taking off would be more difficult. One mistake on your part and four, not two, people would be stranded with no one available to get help.

It does seem a safe bet to return to home base, but it would take time to get there and get help. Meanwhile, Josh and Peter would be in danger. Bandits and smugglers are known to roam the area, not to mention scorpions and poisonous snakes.

The abandoned airstrip on the border is much closer. It wouldn't take long to get there, and you could radio for help then. The food cache is there, too. You could return to Josh and Peter and drop some food and supplies down to them.

If you decide to return to home base for help,
turn to page 18.

If you decide to land immediately,
turn to page 27.

If you decide to go to the abandoned airstrip on the California-Mexico border,
turn to page 33.

"We're heading north, Isabel," you say. "We've got to get help. It's no good having all four of us down there."

"I guess so, but those clouds look bad. They could rip a wing off."

"Look down," you say, tipping the Arcus on its port wing for a better view.

"Gotcha. The land breeze is bad. Landing would be hard," Isabel says.

You kick the plane into a tighter bank and ascend the column of rapidly rising air. The front is almost on top of you now, and there seems to be a path between two huge thunderheads.

"Here we go," you say loudly, remembering that the intercom is out.

The Arcus 12 skims along and climbs rapidly, headed for the twisted clearing between the clouds. The wind buffets the aircraft, and the wings shiver in the strong gusts.

"Hold on, Isabel! Hold on!"

There is a tremendous upsurge of air, and the Arcus rises rapidly for what seems like forever. Your ascent is followed by a sudden drop, as if a large hand had reached out and slapped you back toward land.

Turn to page 21.

"I say we head back to our airfield. Once we're down, we might not be able to get back up."

"Okay," Isabel says. She is peering down at the silver-winged plane on the desert below.

To give you both a better view, you bank the Arcus 12 and descend at the same time. The altimeter spins slowly down, finally showing one thousand feet. From this height you can make out the plane quite clearly. Peter and Josh are outside waving at you.

"What do you think, Isabel? Are they all right?"

"They look okay to me," she replies.

Go on to the next page.

A quick glance at the variometer, the instrument that shows thermal action, makes you nervous. The upward-moving air is not half as active as it was before. You tighten your bank, looking for the thermal, but it is no good. You are losing altitude.

"Back to power, Isabel. Ready?"

"Roger. Gas tank switched on. Reserve tanks off and full," she replies.

"Here goes," you say as you hit the starter button. The Limbach engine kicks over and sputters as a puff of bluish smoke spits out of the exhaust port.

"Too much choke," Isabel comments. "Careful."

Turn to page 20.

"Darn it," you mutter. "This thing won't start."

The propeller spins in jerky fits, then catches as the engine fires and holds. You watch the RPMs build nicely, and you are relieved.

"Watch the airspeed," Isabel says over the intercom.

"No problem," you reply, watching the airspeed slowly increase from sixty knots to close to eighty-five knots. You tighten the bank, and the plane soon sits at an altitude of 1745 feet.

"How do we tell them what we're going to do?" Isabel asks.

"We'll circle. I'll drop down, you point north. They'll get the idea. If there's anything wrong, they'll let us know."

"I say we hang around for fifteen minutes or so. They can write a message in the sand if they need to."

"Okay, Isabel, but we don't have unlimited fuel."

Turn to page 22.

Fighting the controls with all your skill, you succeed in bringing your plane back to a fairly level and normal mode. But that doesn't last long—the storm is all around you. Soon the Arcus is swallowed by the white and gray thunderheads.

Droplets of moisture coat the canopy. There is a moment of calm, and you glance at your altimeter.

"Yikes! We gained four thousand feet just then! That's crazy! We're being sucked into the center of this storm cell!" There's no escape. No ejection seat. A parachute would be torn to shreds in an instant even if you had one. Your fragile craft is headed straight into a vortex of roiling black clouds.

"Isabel, we're—"

Moments later debris from the dismembered Arcus flaps down to the hilly, brown, dry earth below. The thunderheads and powerful Nature have won another round in man's constant challenge to defy earthbound limits.

The End

The air in the cockpit suddenly seems hot to you. You ease open the small vent in the canopy, and a cooling draft enters the cabin. On the sand below you see Josh and Peter making huge letters. Dragging their feet, they create a big OK. Isabel motions to them from the port side of the cockpit as you dip down for a pass over them. She points north.

"Once more?" you ask.

Go on to the next page.

CHOOSE YOUR OWN ADVENTURE® 23

SILVER WINGS

BY R. A. MONTGOMERY

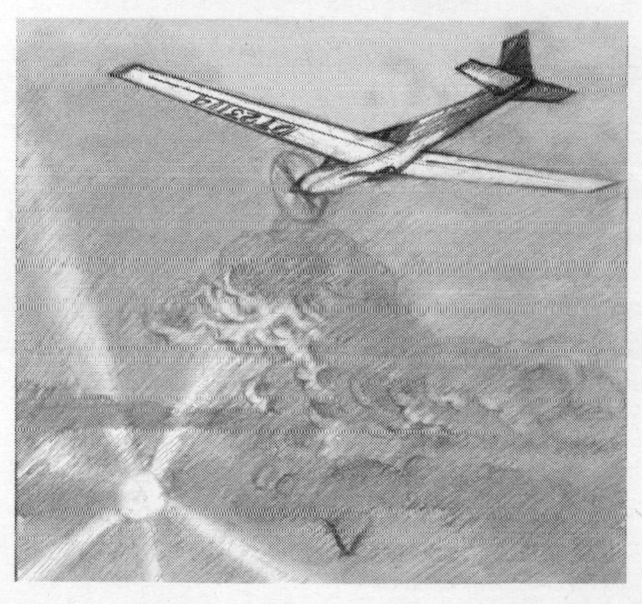

ILLUSTRATED BY VLADIMIR SEMIONOV

CHOOSE YOUR OWN ADVENTURE® CLASSICS
A DIVISION OF

CHOOSECO
WAITSFIELD, VERMONT

Illustrated by: Vladimir Semionov
Book design: Stacey Boyd, Big Eyedea Visual Design

For information regarding permission, write to:

CHOOSECO®
P.O. Box 46
Waitsfield, Vermont 05673
www.cyoa.com

ISBN-10 1-933390-23-9
ISBN-13 978-1-933390-23-9

Published simultaneously in the United States and Canada

Printed in the United States of America

0 9 8 7 6 5 4 3 2

"No good," Isabel replies. "It's our radio not theirs. The darn thing's dead. And I mean dead."

Glancing at your instruments, you are shocked to see them inoperative, except for the altimeter and the compass, neither of which needs electrical power. At that precise moment, the engine sputters, slows, and then quits. This time the silence is ominous, not comforting.

"Can you hear me, Isabel?!" you shout back at her.

"Yes, but just barely. What now?"

The altimeter shows that you have actually risen four hundred feet in the last several minutes. You are banking into a thermal, riding the lift. Without the altimeter it can be very hard to judge altitude. While the worry is usually losing altitude, you know cases of pilots lifted so high lack of oxygen became a serious issue.

"We can land or I guess we can try to make it back to base or some other landing field on wind power. Somebody has got to report what's going on," Isabel says.

"Yeah, you're right, but we've got weather moving in," you say, looking out the front. Ahead hovers a huge mass of cumulonimbus clouds, thunderheads, blocking the northern sky. Glancing at the ground, you see wind kicking up small dust devils. Josh and Peter are taking shelter in the Arcus. If the clouds weren't so dangerous, they'd be beautiful, boiling and tumbling ever higher into the stratosphere.

Turn to page 26.

"This is scary, Isabel. This is getting really scary," you confide in your friend. You know as the pilot in charge you should put at least a brave face on it.

"What should we do?" she asks anxiously.

"We can land or we can try for that field in Red River," you offer. "It's not too far."

"Either way is iffy," she replies. "We have no engine, and landing could be dangerous."

What should you do?

If you decide to keep on heading north for the field at Red River, engine or not, turn to page 17.

If you decide to land immediately, turn to page 39.

"I sense real danger here," you say to Isabel. "One plane down and looks like we're going to be next. It's best to stay together."

"I agree. Let's do it."

The land below does not look at all inviting. Josh and Peter made it, but they didn't have much room to spare.

"Hey, look. They're waving us off," Isabel says, looking down.

Sure enough, Josh and Peter are frantically waving to make sure you don't land in the same spot.

"I really wish they had a radio," you say, desperate.

"Well, they don't, and we've got to get down. How about over there, beyond that rise in the land?"

"We'll check it out," you reply, scanning the terrain below and to the right of where Peter and Josh are standing.

Turn to page 28.

After about two miles the land seems to flatten somewhat. There are two ridges of hills between them, but they don't seem likely to create a major problem. The Pacific Ocean glints far off to the right.

"We can hike this land, don't you think, Bel?" you ask.

"Well, things on the ground are never the same as they look from the air," she replies.

"We really don't have a choice. Let's take another look."

At that moment, your engine sputters and dies.

Go on to the next page.

"Isabel, we're in trouble."

"Not yet. This thing's a glider, remember?"

"Yeah, but we have just one chance. We can't go around again."

"We can. There's enough thermal activity to give us time. Just put it down nice and easy."

You put the Arcus into a sweeping bank and survey the terrain below. From your position it looks rough but possible: scrub brush, some nasty looking rocks, a small hill here and there, and a bunch of dried-up trees near where you want to land. There isn't much of a choice.

"Look up," Isabel says.

"Roger," you reply, taking a quick glance through the Plexiglas canopy. What you see is not in the least bit comforting. Huge banks of thunderheads have filled the sky to the north.

"This is not our day, Bel. Where did they come from?"

"They were mentioned on the weather report. Just got here sooner than we thought."

"Well, here goes. We have to get down."

Turn to page 31.

Concentrating with all your might, you survey your landing area and set up the approach as best you can.

"Flaps down, Bel. We're going in."

"You're doing great, pal, just great. No problem," she replies.

The ground is coming up fast. Bushes, scrub, and rocks start to appear large and menacing. A crosswind tears at the Arcus, trying its best to throw you off course and send you crashing onto the rough, desert land. You are below the level of the surrounding hills. Your airspeed is right around sixty knots.

There is a bubble of rough air, and the Arcus jumps a bit. You pull back ever so slightly on the stick. The nose rises a hair, and the Arcus flares and finally settles to earth. The wheel on the port side digs into the sandy terrain, then breaks loose, and the Arcus bumps heavily down the sand. You try not to fight the controls, but instinct makes you apply too much brake, and the Arcus pivots and slews violently to the side.

"We're down!" you yell.

The Arcus has come to a smacking halt.

Turn to page 32

"What did you think of that, Bel? Not bad, huh?"

There is no reply.

"Isabel? Hey, Isabel, don't play games."

Still no reply.

Turning around, you see Isabel slumped forward, her head on the instrument panel.

"Isabel!" you shout, fighting to break free of your safety harness. The straps unbuckle, but you have some trouble with the canopy. It seems jammed. Finally the latch snaps open, and the canopy slides back. A wave of warm desert air rushes in.

Pushing up from your seat, you leave the cockpit and slide to the ground, moving along the fuselage to Isabel. She is unconscious, breathing in short, shallow gasps. Her face is pale, and her forehead cool and moist. You see no sign of injury, no welts or gashes that might indicate she was hurt during the landing.

You can make Isabel as comfortable as possible in the cockpit. Other than that, you don't know what to do for her mysterious unconsciousness.

You really need to get help. But you're nervous about leaving her alone.

If you decide to leave Isabel and go to Josh and Peter for help, turn to page 50.

If you decide to stay with her, turn to page 46.

"Isabel, I think it's best to get to that old airfield. It's nearby, and we've got food there. We can use that as a base of operations. Two downed planes are a lot worse than one. If we land where they did, our chances of being able to take off again aren't good."

"You're the pilot in command," she replies. "But to tell you the truth, I agree with you one hundred percent. I hate thinking of those two down there, but let's do what we have to do."

You study the ground below wondering if maybe there is another landing place after all. You spot what looks like a single file of some thirty people walking. You point them out to Isabel.

Turn to the next page.

"They're not out for a picnic. Must be migrants heading for the border. I wouldn't want to be in their shoes. Good chance they'll get robbed by coyotes," Isabel remarks.

You know about those coyotes, worse than the animals of the same name. They guide migrants over the border for a price and often rob them and abandon them. But there's nothing you can do about that right now.

You scan the sky, noting banks of high clouds—thunderheads. Hidden within them is the force to rip the wings off your plane. You swivel around, taking in the whole sky. It's clear to the south and east, but the north and west are a cluster of clouds.

"Bel, we've got trouble. Take a look."

"I already have. We've got time, not much, but we'll make it. Turn that engine on and let's go."

"Roger," you reply, hitting the start button. You have a few moments of anxiety as the engine balks at the start command. Finally it catches.

Go on to the next page.

You skim along right under the cloud base at an altitude of about five thousand feet. The air is bumpy, and you must keep a firm hold on the controls without overpowering them. Intent on your job, you keep communication between you and Isabel to a minimum.

Miles slip by, and Isabel does the navigating, giving you the compass heading and the corrections for wind drift. Luck is with you, and the clouds do not dip down to engulf you. You share a quick lunch of sandwiches and juice from Isabel's lunch bag.

An hour later, Isabel announces, "This radio's dead. Must be the same kind of electrical quirk that Josh and Peter had. Hey, you don't think it's sabotage, do you?"

Turn to page 36

"Sabotage! I doubt it. I'm sure it's just mechanical. These two planes are new—same model, same manufacturer, same avionics. There's a screwup somewhere, but no sabotage. I promise you."

After another twenty minutes, Isabel points below. "We're there. We did it! We got there! Look to the port side. That's the field!"

Sure enough, below and to the left lies a short runway. It seems isolated and abandoned. There is a small shack at the north end but no vehicles or any sign of people. You bank the Arcus into a slow turn.

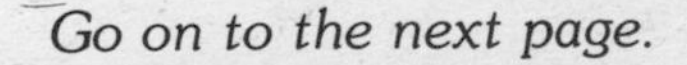

Go on to the next page.

"Looks good to me," you say.

There is no reply. Removing your headset, you shout to Isabel. "Hey, Bel, the intercom is out. We'll have to talk loud. Okay?"

Only silence returns. Turning around, you see Isabel bent forward, clutching her middle. Her face is pale, and her eyes are squeezed tightly shut.

"Isabel, what's the matter?" you exclaim.

She groans. "My stomach, it hurts," she manages to say. "I'm nauseous and my head is killing me."

Just as you reach for an air sickness bag to hand her, she moans softly and slumps forward onto the instrument panel. She's unconscious!

The radio is out, clouds are building, Isabel is in trouble of some kind, and the airfield below shows not a sign of human life.

Turn to page

Your thoughts whirl frantically, but you manage to calm down enough to formulate a plan. You could make a dash for Arbor Field, your home base, but that direction is right where the clouds are coming from. Isabel is in trouble of some sort—perhaps it might be wisest to get down right away and see if you can find help.

If you decide to head for home base,
turn to page 60.

If you decide to land immediately,
turn to page 66.

"We'll never make it through those clouds, Isabel. They'll rip our wings off. Down we go."

"Yeah, well, be careful. That's tough going down there. Hey! Where is it?"

"What? Where's what?"

"The land. We're in the clouds. I can't see ground."

"We'll circle, then I'll test the bottom of the clouds."

"You know we're somewhere near Punta Rheta. Some of these hills go up to almost two thousand feet. Careful," Isabel says.

"Roger. Our altitude is close to four thousand feet right now. We've got room to spare," you say.

It's really tough flying in the clouds without full instruments. You don't know which way is up, and you bounce around like a rubber ball, your stomach heaving. Vertigo takes over and you fight the feeling as best you can.

"I'm going to try it," you yell to Isabel.

"No, not yet. Keep going," she replies.

You try to keep the Arcus flying in what you think is a level mode. But suddenly you are hit by a violent smack of wind, and the fragile craft shudders sideways through the rough air.

Turn to page

The wind acts like a vengeful force, punishing you for coming up into its domain. First you are slithering sideways, then you are bounced up and down, then you fall like a rock only to be thrown upward. Your controls seem useless. You are in the heart of the storm. Rain, swirling wind, and clouds surround you.

"Holy moly, look!" Isabel shouts, her voice barely audible above the roaring of the wind.

"Where?" you ask.

"There!"

Below and to the right is a patch of clear sky, like a special door open only to you. Below that is the cruel land of the Baja California peninsula.

"Now or never, Bel," you say, pushing the stick forward, diving for the cloud break.

Go on to the next page.

"Hold on, we're gonna make it," you say, as you keep the Arcus in its steep dive.

The wind does its best to hold on to you, but you overcome it. Suddenly you slip from the grasp of the storm and are in free air above the dry, brownish land of the Baja.

"Where are we?" Isabel asks.

"Beats me," you reply, happy that you are out of that storm cell.

"Great. We don't have an engine, we don't have much altitude, we don't know where we are, and—"

She stops talking and grabs your shoulder with a jerk.

"Look at that!"

Turn to page 42

You look down and see the ocean. It sparkles in the muted sunlight peeking through the clouds. Its surface is rugged and angry; no craft could survive on it.

"What now?"

"Head to terra firma."

"Fat chance. Look!"

The Arcus banks slowly, and you face a wall of storm clouds, no land in sight. You turn to the almost useless instruments and look at the silent, unmoving propeller. Struggling mightily, you climb a column of rising air and try to keep from being engulfed in the shredded cloud surface once again.

"We'll make it, Isabel. You'll see. We'll make it," you assure her.

Turn to page 44.

You head the Arcus northward, praying that the thermals will be enough to keep you aloft and that the storm won't tear you apart.

For many minutes you and Isabel are silent. You grip the control stick and catch a faltering thermal, which soon dies.

Without knowing exactly when, you realize you're completely free of the storm. The thunderheads have grown smaller, smoother, and they've faded into the south. But land is still out of sight, and the altimeter reads a mere fifteen hundred feet. Below, the sea looks slate gray.

"Look, land!" shouts Isabel, banging on the fuselage.

Go on to the next page.

"All right!" You peer ahead and spot a shimmering strip on the horizon to starboard.

"It's the States," Isabel says. "Look at the beach, and all the cars in the parking lots. It's good old southern California!"

You pick a deserted part of the beach and silently skim to a landing.

Turn to page 7

Your only choice is to stay with Isabel, you decide. After making her as comfortable as possible, checking her vital signs, and assuring yourself there is no more that you can do, you set off to explore the immediate area.

The terrain is bleak, but there is a beauty to it. You wish the four of you were well and enjoying this land together. The morning seems like weeks ago. Only a distant memory remains of the excitement and plans for a trip that was to be so much fun. You try not to waste too much time on regret.

After making two circuits of the area, you are satisfied that it is safe. You gather a heap of firewood for the night and check on Isabel.

To your delight and relief, she is coming around and greets you upon your return.

"Where have you been?" she asks.

Go on to the next page.

"What? Is that you, Isabel?"

"Well, last time I checked it was," she replies.

You know from her response that she is okay.

"Hey, what happened?" you continue.

"I never had anything like that happen to me. Must have been something I ate. Do we have any tea or water or something?"

"Coming right up. This might not be a four-star hotel, but we aim to please."

You busy yourself with the fire, and just soon enough, because night comes fast in the Baja. With it comes a chill, but the fire you made provides some warmth. The water soon comes to a boil, and you make tea. You also cook up freeze-dried chicken soup, some rice, and a slice of fresh ham that you packed this morning.

"What do you think, Isabel? Will you be all right to walk tomorrow?"

"I'm all right now. What do we do about Josh and Peter?"

"We'll search for them tomorrow. I think they're right over that ridge. I could go up there now and see if I can spot a fire or lights from their camp."

Turn to page 4

"Well, maybe it's best to wait for first light. You don't know the area. You could easily get lost in the dark."

It does seem safer to wait. On the other hand, you're worried about Josh and Peter. They might be injured or in danger. Maybe you should try and get to them as fast as possible.

If you decide to search for them tonight, turn to page 75.

If you decide to wait for morning, go on to page 49.

You decide it would be more prudent to postpone your search until morning.

"I'll put some more wood on the fire. You get some sleep, Isabel. I'll keep watch."

"Well, wake me when you're tired. Don't be too much of a hero," she replies.

"Don't worry," you say, feeding the fire with more dry wood.

The evening passes slowly. Around two o'clock in the morning you finally drift off into a half slumber without waking Isabel to take her shift.

A noise interrupts your nervous, dreamless sleep. It's not loud, but it is coming closer. Part of you is frozen in fear. The other part is ready for action. The action part wins out, and you slip away from the fire to hide in the shadows of the Arcus. You pick up a hefty stick and wait.

Turn to page 56.

"Isabel," you say. "If you can hear me, I'm going to get you help." You hesitate for a moment, but there is no indication she's heard. You ease her into a sleeping bag under the wing of the plane, and leave, heavy hearted, in Josh and Peter's direction.

The hills and ridges that you saw from the air look a lot bigger now that you have to cross them on foot. They are steep, rocky, and filled with scrub brush.

"What did I do with that compass?" you ask yourself, fumbling around in the pockets of your flight suit. It is nowhere to be found. Instead of turning back for it, you plunge on ahead. Sweat ripples down your forehead, and you wish that you had changed out of your flight suit into shorts.

It takes more than two hours, longer than you had expected, to get to the top of the first ridge. From the highest point, you survey a bleak picture of even more ridges. It's a long way down and a longer way up the next ridge. Uncertainty floods through you, and you fear for Isabel.

A shadow crosses overhead. Looking up, you see a large bird gliding in circles. It looks as if it is checking the terrain for food.

Go on to the next page.

"Vulture!" you scream. "It's a vulture!" A horrible picture of Isabel picked apart by the hooked beak and sharp talons of this creature frightens you beyond belief. The bird continues its flight, circling in a controlled pattern over the ground. Then, as if beckoned, it swoops off in the direction of the coast. Relief replaces your fear, and with a last look in Isabel's direction, you head down the steep ridge.

"This is going to be a long afternoon," you say to yourself, trying your best to build your courage.

Turn to page 52.

The going is tough, no doubt about it. The sneakers you wore were a good idea for flying the Arcus, but they are inadequate for the task at hand. You stumble on the tough terrain, and your shoes are torn by the jagged rock. The water bottle you carry is heavy, but it is a great comfort to have it.

"It can't be that far," you say out loud, trying to keep your spirits up.

The next ridge is just as hard to cross as the first one, and when you crest that one, there is yet another ridge ahead. Clouds have obliterated the sun, providing some relief from the heat, and the wind has picked up. Swirls of dust blow around you.

Go on to the next page.

"Keep going," you say, encouraging yourself. The image of Isabel lying unconscious and unprotected gnaws at you. You start to doubt your decision to leave her alone, but what could you have done by just staying with her? You'd better just keep going now. You're losing focus and you don't pay attention to your footing. You stumble on a nasty set of rocks. You fall hard, but stand back up uninjured.

Finally you reach a ridge, and there below you is the other Arcus.

"Josh! Hey, Josh! Peter! It's me!" you shout at the top of your lungs. "Hey, you guys, it's me." Your voice echoes.

There is no reply and no sign of your two friends. All is silent and empty except for the wind. Stories of bandits in the Baja suddenly spring to your mind. Small gangs of these men are known to prey on tourists who visit this ruggedly beautiful land. There are stories of people who simply disappear. Instinct warns you to be careful.

Turn to page 5

A rock outcropping offers good cover, and you duck behind it. In your frozen position, a cramp seizes your left leg. Gingerly you move it and massage the strained muscles.

Carefully you peer around the rock outcropping. There is still no sign of life. The Arcus sits on the ground like a discarded toy. Maybe, just maybe, Josh and Peter are out searching for water or surveying the terrain. Maybe there's a note or a clue to what has happened.

You're tempted to go down there and check it out immediately. On the other hand, if you waited until nightfall, you wouldn't risk being spotted by bandits. Maybe you should wait a while.

It's a tough choice. You've already waited cautiously for half an hour. You've even checked your back trail to see if anyone is following you. Everything seems deserted around the Arcus. Maybe it is okay to go down now.

If you decide to go down to the Arcus immediately, turn to page 64.

If you decide to wait for nightfall, turn to page 11.

As minutes go by, the noise becomes louder and closer.

You suck in your breath and wish you could stop your heart from pounding.

You can just make out the outlines of two men. They're coming toward you! You swing the stick with all your might but stop when you hear familiar voices.

"Hey! You almost killed me!" Josh shouts. "It's us! We were just trying to be quiet so we wouldn't wake you two up. Come on. Let's douse the fire. There are some very unfriendly types over on our side."

Turn to page 58.

CHOOSE YOUR OWN ADVENTURE®

DISCOVER INFINITE REALMS™ AT WWW.CYOA.COM

CHOOSE YOUR OWN ADVENTURE®
γ
φ
δ
CHOOSE YOUR OWN ADVENTURE®
γ
φ
δ

The commotion has woken Isabel. Josh and Peter proceed to tell you of their narrow escape from a pair of bandits.

"We were lucky to get away, but we can't stay here for long," Peter says. "Those guys are armed and dangerous."

"But how do we get out of here?" Isabel asks.

"I managed to steal a map from them." Josh pulls it out of his jacket. "It's very detailed, showing all the trails of the area. Look here." Josh points at the map. "We're not too far from this village on the coast."

"We're going to have to leave tonight," Peter adds. "It's a clear night, and the moon's almost full. I think we can find our way. Okay?"

"But Isabel's not feeling too well," you say.

"I can make it," Isabel says firmly.

It's a tough hike, but the four of you reach the village before dawn. Peter and Josh alert the Mexican Federales about the bandits, and you all head home to California. All in all, this was not the vacation you had in mind.

The End

You creep around the rock outcropping and circle out in pursuit of the departing figure. Moving on all fours, you slink from rock to rock.

You don't get far. Within a hundred yards you run into two other men. They are armed and angry.

"Well, well, another rabbit for our pot! Okay, kid, where did you come from? Talk quick or else," one of them says.

"Hey, I'm just out here on vacation. No problem—I'll be on my way. See you around," you say, feeling foolish.

"It's not so easy, my friend. You could bring a good price. Are your parents rich?"

"No, no, not at all. We're poor, very poor," you try to convince them.

"Well, if that's true, that's too bad for you. Come with us."

As they motion with their pointed revolvers for you to walk ahead, you wonder if you'll ever see California again.

The End

"We're going home, Bel. You'll be all right, I promise."

A quick check of the fuel is reassuring. You can make it back with room to spare; that is, if the clouds don't rip you to shreds. With a last look at the deserted field, you head the Arcus northward, upset that two friends are down in rough land and Isabel is unconscious behind you. All the training in the world won't prepare you for the unexpected.

You turn your attention to flying, doing your best to keep focused. Still, you frequently try to get a response from her.

"Bel? Can you hear me? We're doing fine, just fine. I'll have you home in no time."

But there is still no response from Isabel. You're thinking of all sorts of diagnoses—from an epileptic seizure to a brain tumor to poison.

"Poison!" you yell. "Sabotage and poison!"

Go on to the next page.

Your mind jumps back in time. One day, at the airfield, a man failed his pilot's flight exam and was told that he had to change his attitude and sloppy flying habits. Peter had been both fair and firm about the whole thing. The man was taking far too many chances, ignoring standard procedures for takeoff and landing. He was famous for slipping into the landing pattern ahead of other people, more than once causing another plane to abort its landing and go around again. Warnings seemed to mean nothing to him. He had laughed them off.

What was also unacceptable to Peter and the others was his constant teasing of female students. All in all, the man was trouble. Peter had bent over backward to be fair in giving him the flight tests, but everyone was relieved when he failed.

Now you remember the man's bitter words: "You'll be sorry, all of you! Just wait and see. You'll regret this day!" His face was contorted with rage and hatred. The whole scene frightened you and everyone else at the time, but Peter said to forget it.

"Could it be him?" you ask yourself out loud.

Turn to page 62.

You are startled by moaning coming from behind you. It is barely audible over the roar of the engine.

"Bel? Bel, is that you?"

"Yeah," she says weakly.

"You okay, Bel?"

"I . . . I . . . feel terrible. Sick."

"What is it? Food poisoning?"

"I don't know. My stomach feels like it's been beaten with a baseball bat. Where are we?"

"We're heading home, Bel," you say, overcome with relief that Isabel is conscious. "Just hang on, I'll have us there soon."

Go on to the next page.

Later that afternoon you make a smooth landing at the field. Isabel is much better. The two of you arrange a mission with the US Border Patrol to pick up Josh and Peter. The people at the border patrol congratulate you for your bravery and heroism. You're proud of yourself, but you feel that luck was on your side as well.

You think that you will take a break from flying for a while. Next time you might not be so lucky.

The End

"Think of Isabel," you say to yourself. Time is wasting, you think.

Leaving the security of the rocks, you move as cautiously as possible, aware of every variation in the terrain. Your senses feel super sharp.

Nothing moves below. Gaining confidence, you descend quickly and boldly. It takes you about twelve minutes to make it to the Arcus.

You are just about to touch the wing of the plane when a man jumps out of a clump of bushes. He is short, dark skinned, bearded, and holding a very mean-looking revolver. The look on his face is one of amusement and fierceness. You stop dead in your tracks.

"So, another one, eh? Well, your two friends will appreciate the company." He laughs.

Go on to the next page.

You couldn't say a word if you tried to—your voice is frozen in your throat. You rack your brain for a way to escape, but you aren't going to argue with this intimidating man. You are stuck.

"Right this way. No waiting," the man says, resuming his guttural laughter.

Newspaper and TV reports carry stories about the search for two motor gliders and their occupants for almost a week. The Mexican and US governments launch a massive joint search. It is eventually given up, however, and the whereabouts of the pilots of these silver-winged gliders is never determined. Your story joins those of Amelia Earhart and Antoine Saint-Exupéry—just one more mystery in aviation history.

The End

You make one last pass over the field to check for obstructions. It looks pretty clear, and you swoop into a final approach. The wind is mild, but this is a crosswind landing, and you are careful and respectful of its power.

Bump! Bump, bump, bummmmp. The Arcus touches down, bounces, and rolls to a stop with plenty of room to spare. Feeding in some power, you taxi the silver-winged plane toward the weather-beaten shack at the north end of the strip.

There are fresh tire tracks in the sand, and you feel a rush of hope and expectation.

"We're down, Bel. Just wait, I'll take care of you. We'll be fine. Don't worry."

The canopy slides back easily, and you climb out of the Arcus. You move toward Isabel and check her vital signs.

"You are one sick pup," you say out loud.

"What's that?" comes a voice from behind you. You freeze for a moment, not knowing whether it's friend or foe. Strange things happen out here in this remote and lonely land.

Slowly you turn around. In front of you stands a short, bearded man in his sixties. He is dressed in neat but old, patched clothing.

Turn to page 101.

With great gentleness, you and your new friend Gonzales remove Isabel from the cockpit of the Arcus. Carefully you carry her toward the shack.

Parked under the shade of a group of scraggly trees next to the shack is a banged-up old pickup truck. Spread out from the cab is a tarp that serves as a tent of sorts. Underneath is a cot and a neat collection of boxes, a camp chair, a radio, and cooking equipment. This must be Gonzales's home, you assume. A small dog is tethered to one of the tarp poles. He is sandy colored, and his tail wags like a propeller so much it's a wonder the pooch doesn't take off.

"Welcome to La Hacienda Gonzales. We'll put your friend here on the cot. Now for some water." Gonzales moves quickly to a barrel behind the old shack. He returns with a jug of water, and moistening a small piece of clean towel taken from one of the boxes, he bathes Isabel's forehead. Carefully he examines her eyes and takes her pulse for a long time. Isabel moves slightly on the cot. This is the first sign of normal behavior, and you feel a rush of hope.

"Your friend does not appear to be seriously ill. She seems to be in a deep sleep."

Turn to page 70.

"How can you tell?" you ask.

"Too many years of experience," he answers.

With a cup of water in your hand, you move over to Isabel and sit by her side, taking her hand in yours. Gonzales stands behind you, sipping some cold coffee.

The pooch strains at its tether in an attempt to get to its master. Finally Gonzales gives in and unties the dog.

Go on to the next page.

Before long, Isabel turns over, opens her eyes, and moans.

"Isabel! Isabel, it's me. Are you okay?" you ask, relieved that she is finally conscious.

"I feel horrible. Absolutely horrible," she says quietly. "Where are we?"

"At the abandoned airfield, the old emergency strip near the border. This is Gonzales, the caretaker Peter told us about. You've been out for about an hour and a half. I've been scared to death about you."

She turns to receive a cup of steaming herbal tea from Gonzales. The dog at his side has finally calmed down.

Turn to page 72.

"Take this, young lady. I know it will help you. I, Don Diego Arturo Jaime Escalante Burgos de Aragon, personally guarantee it," he says.

She sips at the hot liquid, makes a face, and says, "What is this?"

"A tea from the desert. It will release all poisons from your system. Drink all of it."

"Do you think I was poisoned?" Isabel asks.

"*Si,* it appears so. You have symptoms of food poisoning. Anything strange to eat today?" Gonzales asks.

"Well, no, but . . . there was a sandwich in the lunch bag that was different from those we usually make. I don't know, it tasted all right."

Go on to the next page.

"You're fine, Señorita, I would not worry much," Gonzales reassures Isabel.

"What about Peter and Josh?" Isabel asks, sitting up and finishing her cup of tea.

"Right where we left them," you reply. "Do you have a radio, Mr. Gonzales?" you ask, hoping against hope that he does. "Maybe I can round up some more help."

"I only have a transistor," Gonzales answers. "A radio to talk with the outside world, no. But show me on this map where your friends are. Perhaps I can help."

Gonzales produces a much-folded and weathered topo map from the glove compartment of his truck. It only takes you a few minutes to orient yourself, and you point to a spot on the map.

"There. That's where they went down. I am sure of it. I saw it from the air and checked the coordinates and the landmarks. That's where they are."

Gonzales studies the map carefully for several minutes. He examines the sky for another few minutes and then speaks.

Turn to page 78.

You decide now is as good a time as any to begin your search. You reassure Isabel you won't be long and set out.

The moon is not too bright, but it does peek through the storm clouds, just enough that you can see where you're walking. Carefully you thread your way up the spiny ridge, saving your flashlight for more difficult spots and in case you need to signal to Peter and Josh. At the top of the ridge, you take a last look back at the fire by Isabel and the Arcus. You plunge down the slope, just keeping your balance until you make it to the bottom of a canyon. Even in the faint moonlight you can see a trail. You walk for a few minutes until you think you hear voices. They echo off the canyon walls so that you can't tell where they're coming from. You round a corner to face a large group of seated huddled figures. Three men with pistols circle the seated captives. You duck behind a rock. The men are coyotes, people who smuggle immigrants into the US. They are systematically robbing each person. They force some to take off their shoes and empty their pockets, looking for cash or gold. Any resistance is met by a threatening gesture with a pistol. Out of perverse cruelty, they empty all the water containers.

Turn to page 76.

The three coyotes, loaded up with their haul, disappear into the night leaving their victims to fend for themselves without a guide and without enough food and water.

You walk into this scene of desperation and despair. It's quickly evident you're not a coyote but a foreigner from the North—a savior. They crowd around you all talking at once. Finally you find one man, Felipe, who speaks some English. You slowly come to understand that these people were led here under the promise of being sneaked into the United States, then robbed and deserted miles from their homes.

You give Felipe a map and the two of you organize the able-bodied, picking diverse routes to go for help. Those going for help disappear into the night. You help the robbed people through the night hoping to encounter help, not more bandits, as the sky brightens to dawn.

The End

"I know the place. It is awkward to get to, but there are two possibilities. First, we can use my truck. The track to this spot is not a good one, but it is not impossible."

"What is the other way?" you ask.

"I happen to be the captain of my very own *La Vida*. She's a humble ship, of course, but seaworthy. It is not far—a matter of minutes. We can go by sea and then hike to where they are. The hiking will be a bit difficult, but it will probably be faster than by truck."

You wonder about the choice. Yes, speed is important and going by boat may be faster.

And yet, the sea may be treacherous, and you're not sure you're up to the hike afterward. The truck will take you directly there. Perhaps land is the way to go.

If you decide to go by land, turn to page 94.

If you decide to go by sea, turn to page 85.

You decide to wait and keep an eye on the Arcus. The man who left does not return, and the blond-haired man has apparently decided to take a late afternoon *siesta*. He spreads out a ground cloth and stretches out beneath one of the wings. When it appears that he's sound asleep, you decide to creep up and figure a way to put him out of action.

You head down the hillside, keeping as low to the ground as possible, taking cover behind bushes and rocks. It's not an easy task, and with the fatigue of the long day setting in, it is rough going.

Turn to page 80.

Finally you are just ten yards from the aircraft. You move only every thirty seconds or so, and the sleeper sleeps on.

You figure that the best way to proceed is to pretend that you have a weapon and wake your captive with a loud and firm command, staying behind the fuselage of the Arcus so that he won't see that you are unarmed. It's a simple plan, but you'll have the element of surprise and avoid the risk of using force.

First, you'll need to disarm him. Screwing up your courage, you slowly walk toward him.

Just then the blond-haired man leaps up from the ground cloth. Startled, he reaches for his weapon.

"Don't try it! Kick it over here, under the plane, or you're a dead man."

"Hey, okay. It's cool. Here comes the gun." He kicks the rifle toward you.

Go on to the next page.

"Now your knife. Drop it on the sand," you order.

He obliges, and with your heart in your throat, you walk around the side of the Arcus with a rope in your hands. The man stays put, but you don't trust him for a second.

"Arms behind your back. Legs spread. Lean forward," you tell him.

Amazingly, the man obeys without a fight, and you quickly cinch his hands with the rope.

"Now we're going to have a little talk," you say.

"I didn't do nothing. What's this all about, huh? I was just guarding this plane against robbers, *banditos,* you know," he says, but you don't believe him for a minute.

"Well, we'll just find out about that? Where's the other guy?"

He squirms on the sandy soil, trying to reposition himself. "What other guy? I never saw nobody, it's just me out here."

"What are you doing out here all alone, then?"

"I'm on vacation. Yeah, that's it. A little camping out, a little surfing, a little hunting. Just me and my 4 x 4. Check it out. My four-wheel drive is just over the ridge."

Turn to page 82.

"I believe you about as much as I believe in the Easter Bunny. Talk or else," you say, not knowing what the "or else" could possibly be.

"Hey, listen, I told ya, I'm on vacation. Nothing more."

"Where are they?" you demand violently.

"Who?"

"I've had enough of you!" You shout with frustration.

"Easy, old buddy," comes a voice from behind you. Your heart almost stops, but then you recognize the voice. It's Josh!

"Josh, Peter! Is that really you?"

As soon as you ask the question, Josh and Peter step into view.

"Boy, am I glad to see you two," you say, breathing a loud sigh of relief. "What happened?"

"Nothing much. These two guys and some of their friends started to nose around the Arc here, so Josh and I hightailed it for the bushes. They gave up trying to find us and left this goon here to guard the Arc. We snuck back and found you'd captured him."

Go on to the next page.

"Watch it," the blond man says.

"We don't want to hear anything from you, bud," says Peter.

"Forget him, you guys. Isabel's hurt," you tell them.

"Hurt? How bad? Shouldn't we get to her right away?" Josh asks frantically.

"Calm down. Let's talk over here," Peter suggests, and the three of you move out of earshot of your hostage.

You explain what happened and where the plane and Isabel are. Then an idea hits you—why not "borrow" the four-wheel drive? It sure would be easier than setting out on foot. But then again, you might draw too much unwanted attention to yourself. Although the 4 x 4 would give you more mobility, you won't be able to maneuver it easily on the rough terrain. Maybe you should just set off on foot.

If you decide to make off with the 4 x 4, turn to page 88.

If you decide to go on foot, turn to page 107.

LA VIDA

"The sea sounds easier, to me," you say.

"Well, now that's decided, *vamanos*. You, Isabel, if you are feeling unwell, there is a cabin on my small boat. It has a bunk bed, and you will be safe. So now, *adelante*."

Gonzales starts up the old truck, which bangs and puffs and then runs. You hope that *La Vida* is in better shape than this relic.

It doesn't take long to get to the dock. It sits on a beautiful inlet, protected from the heavy sea by a ridge of rock. The water is a dazzling blue-green, clear enough to see the bottom. The boat rides at anchor a few feet off the dock. It's a beautiful boat, about thirty feet long, broad of beam, wooden construction, obviously an old fishing boat, well maintained and well loved.

Turn to page 86.

"All aboard, as you say," Gonzales shouts. He slaps a faded and crumpled captain's hat on his head.

Gonzales rows out to his pride and joy in a small dinghy. With the three of you plus *Perrito Caliente*, the small dog, there isn't much space between the gunwales and the water. You'd love to go for a swim, the water is so inviting. Maybe there will be time for that later, but now it is important to get to Josh and Peter.

Captain Gonzales fusses about *La Vida*, then checks all lines both fore and aft. Finally he pushes the starter. There is an immediate response from the twin diesel engines, and the reassuring sound of well-serviced equipment is an encouragement to both you and Isabel.

"She'll make sixteen knots. Quite a bit for an old boat, but she's good," Gonzales announces with pride. "Cast off fore and aft," he commands, expecting both you and Isabel to know and follow his commands. He is not disappointed. Moments later, the boat leaves its anchorage and heads for the open sea.

"Here, look for yourself on this chart. We will go first around this headland and then make straight for the shore where we can approach your friends by foot. I predict that with fairly good weather we will be there in six hours."

Go on to the next page.

The boat wallows a bit in the waves as it enters the unprotected water of the Pacific Ocean, and at first you are apprehensive. But it doesn't take you long to get the feel of being afloat, and you like it.

"Take the wheel and keep this compass heading." Gonzales tells you. "Señorita Isabel, go below and sleep." Isabel doesn't argue and heads for the comfort of the bunk. You listen to Gonzales and take the wheel.

The time passes quickly. You love the sea, the smell of salt air, even the jolt when a big wave hits you broadside. You feel at home on the water just as you do in the air. Keeping a close eye out, you spot a storm brewing on the horizon, just as Gonzales points to your landfall.

Twenty minutes later, you drop anchor, and the three of you and *Perrito* head in the dinghy for shore. The first drops of rain hit and the wind whips up the ocean. But you make it onto the beach with little incident.

"I calculate we're about three kilometers from your friends. It's rough even without the rain, but we'll make it. *Vamanos,*" Gonzales says.

Turn to page 104.

"I think we should take this guy's 4 x 4," you say to Josh and Peter. "We've got to get to Isabel as soon as possible."

"I don't know, that's theft," Peter says. "We're in a foreign country, and our Spanish isn't going to convince any policeman."

"Well, we could take him along," Josh says.

"Are you nuts or something? First you want to steal his car and then you want to kidnap him. No way!"

"Peter, this is an emergency," you answer.

"Sorry guys, I'm out," Peter says.

"How about Isabel?" you ask.

"We'll do our best," Peter replies.

"Come on, guys, why don't we just ask him. How about that?" Josh says.

Go on to the next page.

"Okay, I'll go for that," Peter says, moving off in the direction of the man sitting on the ground.

You accompany him and begin the questioning.

"Look, maybe we've got you all wrong. Maybe you are on vacation. If so, we need your help. We have to borrow your 4 x 4," you say as nicely as you can.

The man nods. You look around, worried that his friend will return at any time.

"How about it? The 4 x 4?" you ask.

"Okay," he replies. "I'll go with you, if you agree to help me out."

"How?" Peter asks.

"Get me out of here. There's more than just the one guy you saw me with. Don't ask any questions. I'll provide the 4 x 4, you provide the extra people power, and let's make tracks. Those guys are scary."

"It's a deal," you say, looking at Peter and Josh for approval. They both nod.

Turn to page 91.

The 4 x 4 is brand-new. Josh jumps into the front seat. There is a key ring on the floor next to the accelerator. Josh starts the engine. “Let’s go,” he says, slipping the car into gear and sliding out onto the sandy track. “Which way to Isabel?”

“Due north, turn around that ridge, there’s another two ridges beyond that, but we can avoid them. Step on it.”

The 4 x 4 chews into the sandy soil and swerves a bit as Josh accelerates. The blond man sits in the middle of the back seat, his hands still tied. His eyes sweep the terrain in front and to the side. You keep an eye on him—you still don’t trust him completely.

Turn to page 92.

"Oh, no! Look out," Josh yells. Three heavily armed men step out from behind a rock.

"Duck!" Peter yells.

Josh accelerates and the 4 x 4 jumps ahead and bounces over rocks and bushes. The sound of automatic fire punctuates the air. The windshield splinters, but Josh keeps on going.

"Those guys are trying to kill us," you say, panicking.

Suddenly the shooting stops.

"Some friends you got," Josh says to the blond man.

"Like I say, I want out. Those guys shoot to kill. Just get me back home in one piece."

"How'd you get involved?" you ask.

"I was dumb. Greedy too, I guess."

Josh keeps on going, and you turn the first ridge, race down a relatively clear stretch, see two more ridges, and turn those as well. The track is rough and difficult, but Josh handles the 4 x 4 well. In another twenty minutes you reach a familiar landmark.

"We're almost there. Step on it, Josh," you say.

Go on to the next page.

Then there they are, the silver wings of the Arcus, and standing beside the fuselage is Isabel. She waves at you. A rush of emotion overwhelms you—she's all right.

Two hours later, the 4 x 4 approaches a small town. You contact the Mexican police and direct them to the two gliders, warning them about the group of bandits. Thanks to the help of the blond man, they are able to round them up. In return for his help, the authorities go easy on the blond man. You're relieved, and you plan to lie low for a while. In a single day you've had enough adventure for a lifetime.

The End

"Mr. Gonzales, I think it would be best to go by truck," you say.

"It is your choice, my young friend."

You bring Isabel along also, reluctant to leave her alone at the abandoned airfield. The truck starts reluctantly, but at last you are off over bumpy terrain.

From your point of view, there doesn't seem to be any sense to the way you are heading. There is no road or discernible track out here in this near-desert land. It doesn't seem to bother Gonzales. He whistles and hums as he maneuvers the old truck around difficult spots. You wonder whether or not this is some strange plot to kidnap you and Isabel. But as soon as the thought appears, you discard it. You are sure that Gonzales is what he seems to be, a kind man who chooses to live apart from the mainstream of humanity.

"There. There is the last big obstacle," Gonzales says, pointing to a spiny ridge rising up in front of the old truck. "We can't cross it, and it is too long to go around. But by foot, it won't be long."

"Great, let's get going," you say. "Okay, Isabel?"

Turn to page 97.

"Follow the tracks," Gonzales urges, but you have already figured that out.

From high on the ridge comes the whine of bullets. They're firing at you! Your shoulder stings. You've been hit! Gonzales checks your wound. "You've been grazed, my friend. It's just a scratch—not to worry."

"Make tracks, buckaroo!" Josh shouts.

It doesn't take long to get out of their range, and soon the five of you and *Perrito* are comfortably driving through the countryside, headed for the airfield.

"I hope those guys don't have wheels," Peter says.

"They won't come near me," Gonzales says in his calm voice. "They are afraid of this old man," he continues, giving a small chuckle. "Tomorrow we will organize the rescue of your aircraft. Tonight we will all relax. I think we've all had enough excitement for one day."

The End

"Yeah, I guess so," Isabel replies. "I don't feel really all that great, but I'll go."

"Hey, why not stay here? What do you think, Señor Gonzales? It'll be safe, won't it?"

"Well, perhaps, but these are difficult lands. There could be dangerous people out here. One never knows. Yet we will be gone only a hour and a half perhaps. So, yes, I guess she could stay. *Perrito Caliente* will defend her. Won't you, *Perrito?*" Gonzales says to his dog, who has taken a great liking to Isabel. He barks in reply.

"Okay, Bel, we'll be back soon. Any trouble, just take off in the truck and head back to the airfield, or hide and wait for us."

"Thanks. Don't be long, please."

"We won't," you say, as you and Gonzales head off for the ridge.

Turn to page 99.

It doesn't take long to make it to the top, and from there you see the narrow valley and the Arcus tipped over onto one wing.

Suddenly you spot Josh and Peter, running as hard as they can. Right behind them are two men with weapons. The sharp ping of rifle fire penetrates the air.

"What's going on?" you shout.

"*Banditos.* Or drug runners. They don't know the word mercy. Quick, we must get your friends to come to us," Gonzales says, standing up and shouting, waving his hands. "Show yourself so they will recognize us."

Turn to page 100.

Jumping to your feet, you shout and wave your arms.

"Josh, Peter. It's me. This way. Hurry!"

A flurry of bullets from small-arms fire whiz over your head. Gonzales pulls you down to the ground.

"That's enough. Let us pray that your friends saw you. We cannot stay here. Maybe the banditos think we have guns and keep away for a while. Let's hope that la Virgen de Guadalupe is with us."

You poke your head around a rock for a peek, and sure enough Josh and Peter are racing your way. They are running in a crouch, taking cover behind rocks wherever they can.

"Josh! This way!" you shout.

Suddenly Josh and Peter come tumbling over the rocks and land on top of you.

"Where in the world did you come from?" Josh pants. "Who's this guy?"

Turn to page 102.

The man looks up at you, smiling. You notice that he has a gold tooth in front. "Can I help you? What's wrong with your friend?" he asks.

"She just passed out. I don't know what's wrong," you say with concern. "Who are you?"

The man moves closer to the Arcus and offers you his hand to shake.

"I am Don Diego Arturo Jaime Escalante Burgos de Aragon," he says.

That has you a bit puzzled. And he speaks so fast.

"You can call me Señor Gonzales for short, or even shorter call me what my amigos do, just Gonzales. But don't call me Speedy, *por favor*. I know I talk fast."

You introduce yourself, realizing that this is the caretaker Peter spoke of. You're in luck.

"Your friend's contact drove in here last week. He left supplies for you and the other plane. They're stored in *mi hacienda*. He explained you might stop."

Your instinct tells you to trust this man. There is a tone in his voice and a look in his eyes that instills you with confidence. You don't have much of a choice, anyway. Here you are with Isabel unconscious, no radio, and Peter and Josh down seventy miles away.

Turn to page 68.

You try to remember Gonzales's full name for Peter and Josh, but Gonzales has to come to the rescue. "Don Diego Arturo Jaime Escalante Burgos de Aragon, at your service."

"What a way to finally meet you," Peter says. "Let's get going!"

"You're right, my friend. *Vamanos!*" Gonzales commands. He is already headed down toward the truck.

When you reach the truck, Isabel, sensing trouble, has it running. She has turned the vehicle around, heading in the right direction. *Perrito Caliente* is at the window, barking.

Go on to the next page.

"Hurry, we must hurry," Gonzales wheezes with the effort of the descent.

Josh is the first to the truck. He throws the door open, happy to find Isabel who's just as happy to find the whole team together again.

Everyone piles in as you head around the truck to driver's side.

"Hit it!" Josh exclaims, as you jump into the driver's seat. Gonzales holds onto *Perrito* tightly.

Turn to page 96.

He didn't exaggerate, it's rough. You finally crest the last ridge in what seems like hours later. Below is the Arcus. No one is around. It's completely deserted, there is an ominous air.

"Josh!" you yell. You feel a strong hand clamp over your mouth.

"Make no sound," Gonzales whispers into your ear. "There is an evil that has walked here. See?" He points at some ugly gashes in the side of the Arcus that you did not see on first glance. Then you notice four neat bullet holes on the fuselage. You search the plane for any clue, even hoping for a possible note from them or at worst a ransom note.

"Your friends are beyond our help. Let us hope that they are not already beyond the help of the Federales or your own border patrol. We will leave now, *con cuidado.* Follow me."

You hate to go, but you trust Gonzales, hoping that Josh and Peter are safe. The best you can do you figure is put in the hands of the authorities, you think.

As you turn away, you can't help but feel that you may never see your friends again.

The End

"Okay, let's walk," you say. "But what about Blondie?"

The roar of a truck a moment later answers your question.

"Hey, he got away!" yells Josh. "Now what do we do?"

"We've got no choice. We've got to get to Isabel, and then maybe we can find help," Peter says.

An hour later, as you struggle along a sandy track on your way back to Isabel, a convoy of Mexican Federales trucks roars up. Isabel is in the lead truck.

"Hi, guys, where ya been?" She says laughing. "We've been rounding up bandits," she adds, pointing to four mean-looking men in the second truck.

You can't help but laugh. It seems Isabel is all right. Not only that, but it looks like she's had an adventure of her own.

The End

CREDITS

Illustrator: Vladimir Semionov was born in August 1964 in the Republic of Moldavia, of the former USSR. He is a graduate of the Fine Arts Collegium in Kishinev, Moldavia as well as the Fine Arts Academy of Romania, where he majored in graphics and painting, respectively. He has had exhibitions all over the world, in places like Japan and Switzerland, and is currently Art Director of the SEM&BL Animacompany animation studio in Bucharest.

This book was brought to life by a great group of people:

Shannon Gilligan, Publisher
Gordon Troy, General Counsel
Jason Gellar, Sales Director
Melissa Bounty, Senior Editor
Stacey Boyd, Designer

Thanks to everyone involved!

ABOUT THE AUTHOR

R. A. MONTGOMERY has hiked in the Himalayas, climbed mountains in Europe, scuba-dived in Central America, and worked in Africa. He lives in France in the winter, travels frequently to Asia, and calls Vermont home. Montgomery graduated from Williams College and attended graduate school at Yale University and NYU. His interests include macro-economics, geo-politics, mythology, history, mystery novels, and music. He has two grown sons, a daughter-in-law, and two granddaughters. His wife, Shannon Gilligan, is an author and noted interactive game designer. Montgomery feels that the new generation of people under 15 is the most important asset in our world.

For games, activities and other fun stuff, or to write to R. A. Montgomery, visit us online at CYOA.com

ADVENTURER'S LOG

ADVENTURER'S LOG

ADVENTURER'S LOG

ADVENTURER'S LOG

ADVENTURER'S LOG

ADVENTURER'S LOG

ADVENTURER'S LOG

ADVENTURER'S LOG

ADVENTURER'S LOG

ADVENTURER'S LOG

ADVENTURER'S LOG

ADVENTURER'S LOG

ADVENTURER'S LOG

ADVENTURER'S LOG

ADVENTURER'S LOG

ADVENTURER'S LOG

ADVENTURER'S LOG

ADVENTURER'S LOG

ADVENTURER'S LOG

ADVENTURER'S LOG

Silver Wings Trivia Quiz

Prove you've earned your Silver Wings
on this adventure through the
Baja Peninsula of Mexico!

1) You and your friends plan a glider flight over the
A. Australian Outback
B. Baja Peninsula
C. French Riviera
D. Suez Canal

2) Your glider is called
A. Dingbat 5
B. Meatball 7
C. Snarkle 10
D. Arcus 12

3) Which of these is NOT part of a motor glider?
A. Fuselage
B. Aileron
C. Transporter Ray
D. Rudder Pedal

4) What does the variometer do?
A. Cooks microwave cheeseburgers
B. Measures height in the air
C. Shows thermal action
D. Lets your mom know where you are

5) When your plane crashes in the desert, you realize you've lost your
A. Marbles
B. Compass
C. Cat
D. Life

6) When Isabel becomes unconscious in the glider, you are lucky to be
A. Rescued by the caretaker of an abandoned airstrip
B. Given a million dollars
C. Also unconscious, so you don't notice
D. Already at the closest hospital

7) Gonzales' dog is named *Perrito*, the Spanish word for
A. Mean dog
B. Little dog
C. Robot dog
D. Crazy dog

8) The "coyotes" you encounter in the desert are actually
A. Wolves
B. Drug smugglers
C. People who smuggle illegal immigrants into the United States
D. Harmless housepets

9) You and Isabel are surprised to learn that Gonzales owns a
A. Jet plane
B. Plasma television
B. Motorcycle
B. Fishing boat

10) When a stranger approaches your campfire, you are ready to attack until
A. You realize it is your friend Josh
B. You are knocked unconscious from behind
C. The fire goes out
D. You decide you don't believe in attacking strangers

ANSWERS

1-B, 2-A, 3-C, 4-C, 5-D, 6-A, 7-D, 8-B, 9-D, 10-B

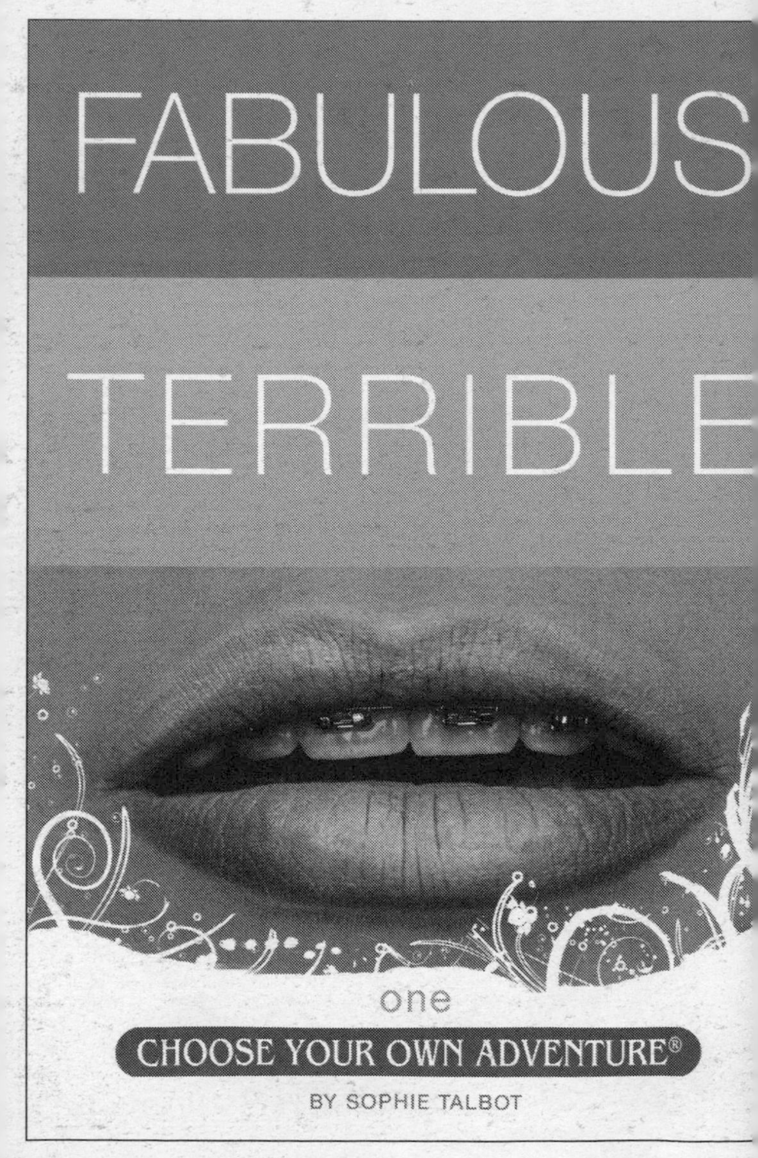
FABULOUS
TERRIBLE
one
CHOOSE YOUR OWN ADVENTURE®
BY SOPHIE TALBOT

Original Fans Love Reading *Choose Your Own Adventure®*!

The books let readers remix their own stories—and face the consequences. Kids race to discover lost civilizations, navigate black holes, and go in search of the Yeti, revamped for the 21st century!

Wired Magazine

I love CYOA—I missed CYOA! I've been keeping my fingers as bookmarks on pages 45, 16, 32, and 9 all these years, just to keep my options open.

Madeline, 20

Reading a CYOA book was more like playing a video game on my treasured Nintendo® system. I'm pretty sure the multiple plot twists of *The Lost Jewels of Nabooti* are forever stored in some part of my brain.

The Fort Worth Star Telegram

How I miss you, CYOA! I only have a small shelf left after my mom threw a bunch of you away in a yard sale—she never did understand.

Travis Rex, 26

I LOVE CYOA BOOKS! I have read them since I was a small child. I am so glad to hear they are going back into print! You have just made me the happiest person in the world!

Carey Walker, 27